Natalie
and the
Thankful Gulls

By Diane LaPierre

Illustration by: Jose Tecson

To order additional copies of this book, contact:
Xlibris
844-714-8691
www.Xlibris.com
Orders@Xlibris.com

ISBN: Softcover   979-8-3694-0047-0
        EBook   979-8-3694-0046-3

Print information available on the last page

Rev. date: 06/23/2023

For my granddaughter, Natalie.
May your journey always be filled with
beautiful shells,
special treasures,
and endless love.

Early mornings were the best time of day for Natalie and Grandma. Together they would walk along the sandy beach, looking for beautiful shells and special treasures.

The salty air would tickle their noses, and the laughing gulls always made them smile.

Natalie had so much fun running with the sandpipers and splashing with the terns.

When she grew tired, she would build sandcastles and wiggle her toes in the sand. She liked watching the birds swimming in the water, flying in the sky, and playing in the sand.

Natalie loved the gulls most of all.

6

"Grandma, listen," Natalie whispered. "I hear chirping."

Quietly, she followed the sound away from the water into the tall beach grass.

She tiptoed carefully near the sand dunes. All of a sudden, she saw two gulls and a nest. She was so excited.

"Grandma, Grandma," she said smiling. "There are three beautiful brown, fluffy chicks in the nest."

"Hi. I'm Natalie," she said to the gulls. "I see you each morning running back and forth in the surf."

"Hi, Natalie. It's so nice to meet you. I'm Mommy Gull, and this is Daddy Gull. We are scurrying to get food for our babies because they are so little. They especially enjoy fish and crabs."

"I can help you get food, too," she said happily.

12

So each day, Natalie and Grandma would gather fish and crabs and place them near the nest.

"Mommy Gull, look," giggled Natalie. "The chicks laugh when I play with them."

Mommy Gull and Daddy Gull were so beautiful with fluffy blue and white feathers. Their tall legs help them to keep a watchful eye on their chicks.

Then one day, Grandma noticed that Daddy Gull's leg was hurt. She looked around until she found a piece of seagrass to wrap around his leg to help it heal.

After a week, he was feeling better and running in and out of the surf getting food.

On this particular day, Natalie was bringing fish and crabs to the nest when she screamed, "Grandma! Grandma! The chicks are gone!"

Grandma hurried. "Yes, the chicks are gone, but, look. There is something very special in the nest."

Natalie ran down to the surf shouting, "Mommy Gull!! Daddy Gull!! The chicks are missing."

Mommy Gull and Daddy Gull laughed. "They are old enough to get their own food now," they said proudly. "We left you beautiful shells to thank you for your help."

"Thank you so much. They are so pretty," Natalie said gratefully.

Now each time Natalie and Grandma walk along the beach, they find a small pile of beautiful shells, and they smile.

Printed in the United States
by Baker & Taylor Publisher Services